PUMPKIN PATCH

by J. P. Press

Consultant: Beth Gambro
Reading Specialist, Yorkville, Illinois

BEARPORT
PUBLISHING

Minneapolis, Minnesota

Teaching Tips

Before Reading

- Discuss the different seasons. What happens in fall?

- Look through the glossary together. Read and discuss the words.

- Go on a picture walk, looking through the pictures to discuss vocabulary and make predictions about the text.

During Reading

- Encourage readers to point to each word as it is read. Stop occasionally to ask readers to point to a specific word in the text.

- If a reader encounters an unknown word, ask them to look at the rest of the page. Are there any clues to help them understand?

After Reading

- Check for understanding.

  ▸ What are some things to do at a pumpkin patch?
  ▸ What can you do with a pumpkin?
  ▸ How does a pumpkin grow? See page 22 for the answer!

- Ask the readers to think deeper.

  ▸ Pretend a friend has never gone to a pumpkin patch. What would you tell them about it?

Credits:

Cover, © Loren L. Masseth/Shutterstock; 3, © Yasonya/Shutterstock; 4, © Zheltyshev/Shutterstock; 5, © Image Source/iStock; 6, © lovelyday12/Shutterstock; 7, © cdrin/Shutterstock; 8, © Chiyacat/Shutterstock; 9, © sonyae/iStock; 10, © Loren L. Masseth/Shutterstock; 11, © Kativ/iStock; 13, © Peter Steiner/Alamy Stock Photo; 14, © Joshua Resnick/Shutterstock; 15, © IvanMikhaylov/iStock; 17, © Brent Hofacker/Shutterstock; 18, © Lordn/iStock; 19, © Billion Photos/Shutterstock; 20, © Le Do/Shutterstock; 21, © FatCamera/iStock; 22, © Stockagogo Photos/Shutterstock; 22, © Paladin12/Shutterstock; 22, © New Africa/Shutterstock; 22, © Amir Photo/Shutterstock; 23, © Robert Winkler/iStock; 23, © Kristina Kokhanova/Shutterstock; 23, © yuris/Shutterstock; 23, © Laura Lee Cobb/Dreamstime; 23, © New Africa/Shutterstock; 24, © -lvinst- /iStock.

Library of Congress Cataloging-in-Publication Data

Names: Press, J. P., 1993- author.
Title: Pumpkin patch / by J.P. Press ; consultant, Beth Gambro.
Description: Bearcub books. | Minneapolis, Minnesota : Bearport Publishing Company, [2021] | Series: Seasons of fun: fall | Includes bibliographical references and index.
Identifiers: LCCN 2020008979 (print) | LCCN 2020008980 (ebook) | ISBN 9781642809367 (library binding) | ISBN 9781642809435 (paperback) | ISBN 9781642809503 (ebook)
Subjects: LCSH: Pumpkin—Juvenile literature.
Classification: LCC SB347 .P74 2021 (print) | LCC SB347 (ebook) | DDC 635/.62—dc23
LC record available at https://lccn.loc.gov/2020008979
LC ebook record available at https://lccn.loc.gov/2020008980

For more information, write to Bearport Publishing, 5357 Penn Avenue South, Minneapolis, MN 55419.

Printed in the United States of America.

Contents

The Pumpkin Patch

It is time for fall fun!

Today, we are going to the pumpkin **patch**.

I am going to pick out a pumpkin.

The pumpkin patch is full.

In summer, farmers planted pumpkin seeds.

Then, the pumpkin plants grew.

They needed lots of sun.

Now, they are big.

Some are long and tall.

Others are short and round.

This one is huge!

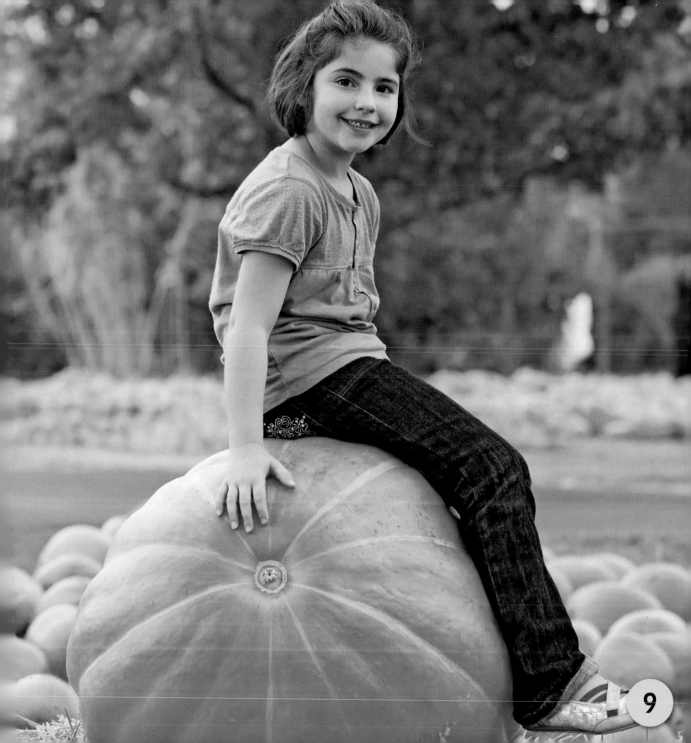

Pumpkins grow on green vines.

I see pumpkins that are green, too.

The green ones are not ready.

I pick one that is orange.

Then, we go on a hayride.

A tractor pulls us along.

There is so much to do
at the pumpkin patch!

When we get home, I scoop out my pumpkin.

I **carve** a big mouth and scary eyes.

My pumpkin will look **spooky** with a light inside!

Pumpkins can be made into many treats.

We **toast** the seeds.

Mmm!

They are salty!

We can bake with pumpkins, too.

Pumpkin cakes and bars are yummy!

I love pumpkin pie.

Visiting the pumpkin patch is fun.

It is one of the best things to do in fall.

How Pumpkins Grow

Pumpkins grow from seeds in the ground. Roots reach down into the soil. A **shoot** pokes up out of the dirt.

Soon, the shoot grows into a long vine with leaves. Green baby pumpkins start to grow from the vine.

Pumpkins on a vine

The pumpkins get bigger. Pumpkins are ready when they are orange all over.

Glossary

carve to cut into a surface

patch an area of land where plants grow

shoot a young plant that has just appeared above the soil

spooky scary

toast to make food crisp, hot, and brown by heat

Index

Read More

Lee, Jackie. *Pumpkin (See it Grow)*. New York: Bearport (2016).

Grack, Rachel. *Pumpkin Seed to Pie (Blastoff! Readers. Beginning to End)*. Minneapolis: Bellwether (2020).

Learn More Online

1. Go to **www.factsurfer.com**
2. Enter "**Pumpkin Patch**" into the search box.
3. Click on the cover of this book to see a list of websites.

About the Author

J. P. Press likes reading, running, and lists of three things. Fall is her favorite time of the year.